ISBN 1-84135-084-2

First published 2001 by Award Publications Limited,
27 Longford Street, London NW1 3DZ

Printed in Belgium

Paper Bears

and the Elephant Who Forgot

by Sue Hall

AWARD PUBLICATIONS LIMITED

One day, Joshua and Tessie, the Paper Bears, were walking in the forest, when they came across something very puzzling. It was an elephant, drawing on the ground with a long stick.

"What *are* you doing?" Joshua asked bravely, for the elephant was much bigger than the Paper Bears and they were scared.

Tessie stood well back, looking over Joshua's shoulder.

"I'm lost," said the elephant. "I've made some marks to help me find my way home, but I can't get any further than this tree."

Feeling a bit braver, the Paper Bears came closer. Tessie looked down. "You're just going round in circles," she said. "Look! There are your footprints."

"They say an elephant
never forgets," said the elephant, with
a sigh. "But I can't even remember which
mark is the last one I made!"

"Perhaps we can help you," said Tessie. "What's your name, Mrs Elephant?"

"Mm, er – just a moment, it's on the tip of my tongue. Oh dear, now I can't even remember my name!"

"We'll give you another name, then," said Joshua.
"How about Dolly?"

"That's a nice name," said the elephant. "I only
hope I can remember it!"

"Why don't you come home with us?" asked
Tessie. "We'll teach you how to remember things."
Dolly thought this was a wonderful idea. Keeping
close behind the Paper Bears, in case she got lost
again, she tramped along after them.

Back at home, Tessie got out lots of paper and a pencil. "We write ourselves notes to remind us of things and pin them where we can see them," she said. "Write 'My name is Dolly'."

"I bet you'll remember it once you've written it down," said Joshua.

"I'll try," Dolly said hopefully.

Joshua and Tessie made themselves a badge each and
wrote their names on them.

"Now you will be able to see which one of us is which,"
said Joshua.

Dolly thought she would write some notes of her own.
"I must get some bananas", said the first one.

Then she wrote: "I must visit my Grandma". But remembering her Grandma made poor Dolly feel very homesick, so she wrote in large letters:
"I MUST REMEMBER MY WAY HOME".

"Don't worry, Dolly," Tessie said kindly. "We'll help you."
So the Paper Bears and Dolly returned to the forest and
found the big tree with the footprints round it.

"Come on, Dolly," said Joshua. "...
...me? Can't you remem...
...y shook her h...
...writt...

Suddenly, the Paper Bears and Dolly heard a rustling and a swishing.

"Look!" shouted Joshua. "The tree's alive! It's bending down and wiping out all your marks!"

"But it's left one," cried Dolly in excitement. "Oh, thank you Big Tree, I remember now! My home is that way."

"Goodbye, Dolly, see you again," said Joshua and Tessie.

"Goodbye," replied Dolly. "I hope I can remember the way back here!"

"Just write yourself a note!" called Joshua, as Dolly tramped happily towards her home.